DIARY OF THE LEGENDARY
ENDER DRAGON

Steve Crafter

Prime Progress Publishing
© Copyright 2015

Editor: Andrew Scott

Proofreader: Pete Stewart

Graphic Designer: Stephen King

Disclaimer:

Thank You For Downloading This Book!

Click Here For More Minecraft Diaries!

Or Go To: http://amzn.to/1KsL9Ie

Table Of Contents

Monday – Entry 1

Tuesday – Entry 2

Wednesday – Entry 3

Thursday – Entry 4

Friday – Entry 5

Saturday – Entry 6

Sunday – Entry 7

Monday - Entry 1

It is a dark and lonely place in the realm where I reside. It is a vast and empty space, with only great towers of obsidian and harsh stone.

Nothing grows here. Nothing lives here. Those who come here surely perish in this harsh, tiny realm I call my home.

I live in solitude and boredom. Only the Enderman alone can withstand living in this terrible place. They alone can withstand my presence.

There are only a few visitors that can make it to the place I call my home. Only a well seasoned veteran of exploration can barely make it to the doorway that would lead them to their end. My end.

Most of them meet their end long before they unravel the mysteries and wonder that is my realm. Some of them wish to just fight me, obtaining vast amounts of glory to their name.

If you are reading this diary it means only one thing.

I have met my END.

Being the guardian of this realm, this is a curious situation for me. Imagine the headlines they will print.

The stories they will tell, even, if you managed to actually defeat a great being such as myself.

"The Great Ender Dragon has met his End!"

What a laugh. No one can defeat me. Even now, as I complete this trivial entry out of boredom, I know that you crossing to my realm alone is an improbable task.

Even now as I lay upon my Obsidian tower, I can feel your curiosity growing. You are searching for me, I can feel it.

You wish to fight me for revenge, for glory, for power. I am filled with rage and excitement all at the same time.

I wonder if you will be able to activate my portal, enabling you to set foot in this plane of existence. Oh how you will rue the day you set foot here in my domain.

I do hope you bring an army with you, or else, my dear friend, you stand no chance against me.

My home is THE END.

It can be your end as well, if you dare to step foot here.

Tuesday - Entry 2

It appears I was wrong about you.

You show such promise, adventurer. Only a brave warrior would dare even try to search for the End Portal at night time.

I am no mere jester, like that Herobrine you fear. In fact, I am even greater than him. Every great warrior dreams of becoming a dragon slayer, and I am such a dragon to slay.

The end to all adventurers! The end to all quests! I must always keep my eye on such promising prospects such as you.

Don't get me wrong, I do not need to keep an eye on you to prepare myself for battle. I am merely bored. That is why I make these entries.

How long it has been since anyone has made it this far! Watching you is the most interesting thing I have seen in a long time!

The ender children follow you in the night and day, reporting your every move. Through their eyes, I see your preparations. I saw your obsidian portal, its beautiful.

It must have taken quite a bit of preparing for. The one place I cannot dwell, the Nether Realm. A fiery place, full of creatures thats attacks would singe the eyebrows off of even the hardiest of warriors.

The perfect hiding place for one of the key ingredients use in activating the dormant portal to my home.

It appears you are truly serious about your choice. This is a good place to train for your inevitable defeat against me.

If you can defeat the keymasters and gain entry to my world, that is.

The terrible and terrifying Blazes. I named them after their destructive attack - which I hoped set you ablaze!

It has been 3 hours since you have set foot into that sinister portal to the Nether realms.

If you cannot survive in there, you have no hopes against me reader. More deadly foes than just the Blaze

wander around in those lands. I hope
you are prepared.

Wednesday - Entry 3

I will tell you a secret, dearest reader. One that you do not know currently in the moment I am writing this. Though, you may have already figured out this secret.

You are not prepared to set foot in my realm.

I will tell you some more secrets.

Obtaining the ingredient from the Nether just now... that is the easiest part of your journey.

Not only is that merely one ingredient of what you need to activate my doorway, you must first locate the portal to reactivate it!

To do just that, you will need the one other ingredient to complete the key. Pearls dropped by my fellow Enderman.

I had entrusted the entire clan of Enderman with these pearls, allowing them to leave my solitary world and visit yours.

It was my gift to them for being able to withstand my presence. I allowed them to leave this place and go elsewhere. That is just how powerful I am.

That should also tell you how powerful they are. The power to be able to blink in and out of existence and go between worlds is a power you can never hope to achieve!

Should you manage to obtain a pearl, you will be able to make an Eye of Ender.

That is the key to my portal, my dear friend and what a secret that is to share with you! Although, I suppose if you are reading this you will already have figured that secret out.

It shall take nine eyes total to activate my portal. Due to the nature of their magic, they can also be used to locate the portal but explode after traveling a short distance during said process.

You can see how this can be problematic for you. Who knows how many total Eyes it can take to find the portal! H

ow many of the Enderman can you actually destroy? My guess at your current state, not many.

Fortunately for you, I will let you in on another secret. Three other adventurers made it here over the centuries.

Long and forgotten, they had come ill prepared for the deadly Stronghold in place to protect my portal.

One of them made it as far as my portal, surviving long enough to place one Eye on its pedestal.

That eye is still there. You only need 8 to go, dear reader. As I write this, you currently have zero.

You may have made it out of the Nether alive. This was a fun game watching you, but the Enderman will take care of the rest.

So sad. I had decided that I would eat you when you arrived, too. It has been so long since I had delivery and

I was so hungry! I guess I could always eat more stone.

Thursday - Entry 4

Well, it appears that luck is on your side, Adventurer. Or would that be considered unlucky?

Every eye you acquire brings you closer to your own end, and today you acquired 4.

I have underestimated you once again. You show as much promise as the last adventurer who made it to my home.

The only thing I know about him was his name, Steve. He introduced himself as he approached my towers of great obsidian, right before I had attacked him. He was barely worthy of me opening my eyes.

You will see signs of his demise, upon entry to my domain. Steve, in an attempt to warn people such as yourself, placed a tacky sign at the entrance.

I left it up as a testament to Steve's tenacity. It makes me chuckle, every time I fly by it.

Beware of Dragon.

Friday - Entry 5

If I could paint a picture for you of my land and I, would you still want to break into this lonely home of mine?

The darkness you see when you close your eyes, that is my sky. Go ahead, close your eyes and look into the sky with me.

Imagine the dark place I live in. Now look down. End Stone, but not like in your land. I live but on a chunk of humble stone. Beyond that, dark black.

On top of the small plot of land where I live, there is a field of Enderman. Each one as bored as I am and looking to protect their home.

You will also see tall, dark Obsidian Pillars. Atop of every Pillar, a crystal made of a material you cannot imagine exists. Each crystal has a piece of my life essence inside.

Each crystal is primed and ready to infuse me again with my life essence if you dare to harm me.

Don't you see? I am invincible in my realm. You are fighting for a dark, lonesome place. Do you still wish to risk it all to come here?

You currently have 10 Eyes. As I sat here in thought, wondering if you will ever make it to my home, you are proving yourself worthy. Once you find the portal, I will be ready.

Saturday - Entry 6

It has been a day that shall be marked down in all of History, here in The End.

You were quite prepared for this. How silly of me not to realize that you never had potential - just information.

You knew of all this already. I look at you now, blue shirt and brown hair. You must be the descendant of Steve.

He must have kept a diary log, such as I, and provided you with the location of the portal and secret to activate it.

I was a fool.

You came in with your army ready to fight. It had been so long since I had visitors, I had gotten bored.

As I toyed with your warriors, alongside my fellow enderman, I did not notice your archers preparing their arrows. I lost 3 of my 5 crystals this day.

That was a good call indeed on your part, dear reader.

An even better call was to have a third team, of builders, to build a small fortress to protect yourself while you rally up against for round two.

As I write this now, I circle your encampment unable to break through the barrier you had created. If you wish to fight come out and fight me, like your ancestor!

I will tell you one last secret, dear friend, there is no fury like a dragons fury. You cannot defeat me. You will meet your end! Even if you win this battle, you cannot win this war.

Sunday - Entry 7

It is a dark and lonely place I live, great adventurer. I live in my end.

You are probably wondering how this entry is appearing before your very eyes. I will explain this all in due time.

I underestimated your wit, reader. You know know that as you read you can see how arrogant I was. I was so sure I was invincible.

I am the mighty Ender Dragon - you are the mighty Ender Dragon Slayer. With my last essence, I imbue my last words to you onto my journal you picked up as the spoils of our little war.

I never saw it coming. You had built what I assumed was protection from my onslaught of attacks.

It was far too late when I realized you had tunneled your way behind my field of vision and knocked out the remaining crystals.

Remember this, you lost merely due to my arrogance. I am the stronger being.

If I had treated you as a worthy adversary and gave it my all... you would be the one who met your end. I learned a very valuable lesson.

But it matters not. Here I am now, stuck in my infantile form. An egg.

Now, I am invincible. There is nothing that can hurt a dragon egg. Here I shall bide my time and strength, waiting for the time when I can be reborn.

I will not take revenge. You won fair and square, dear reader. I will soon resume my lonely existence while you will take on a mantle of great glory.

You have won this time and I yield to your greatness, but you truly have not defeated me.

I always exist. There must always be an END.

PREVIEW OF AMAZON BEST SELLER 'DIARY OF THE LEGENDAY HEROBRINE'

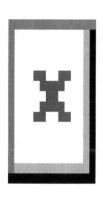

Monday – First Entry

I exist.

My name is Herobrine.

I am everywhere at the same time.

I live in your treasure room, that place where you try to keep all of your most prized possessions safe from harm.

I am in the strongholds you explore and the mines you create. I am watching you when you are scaling small pathways through a treacherous lava pit.

I am the unknown force that causes an onslaught of enemies to appear at your back as you run away from a dark dungeon.

I am the reason you become entombed in gravel while you are trying to dig your mines. You may never know I am there, laughing as you fall into lava or get attacked by my minions.

You may never know it was me, unless you happen to turn around and catch a glimpse of me before I disappear in front of your eyes ... leaving you helpless to your fate.

I do whatever I want. I play for fun and my type of fun is having a minion blow up and destroy the fence that keeps your cattle contained. I enjoy setting your animals free.

I have been slacking off for a while. A voice can be heard in the darkness that begs and pleads my name to be born into their world. I will follow it, I was getting bored here anyway.

Click Here To Read More!

Or Go To: http://amzn.to/1M9z3iH

Thank You For Downloading This Book!

Click Here For More Minecraft Diaries!

Or Go To: http://amzn.to/1KsL9Ie

Made in the USA
Middletown, DE
19 July 2015